STEP 2
READING WITH HELP

DreamWorks

MR. PEABODY & SHERMAN

TIME-TRAVEL TROUBLE!

Adapted by Billy Wrecks

Random House 🏠 New York

Mr. Peabody
is very smart.
He is an inventor.
He is also a dog!

Dear Parents:

Congratulations! Your child is taking the first steps on an exciting journey. The destination? Independent reading!

STEP INTO READING® will help your child get there. The program offers five steps to reading success. Each step includes fun stories and colorful art or photographs. In addition to original fiction and books with favorite characters, there are Step into Reading Non-Fiction Readers, Phonics Readers and Boxed Sets, Sticker Readers, and Comic Readers—a complete literacy program with something to interest every child.

Learning to Read, Step by Step!

Ready to Read   Preschool–Kindergarten
• big type and easy words • rhyme and rhythm • picture clues
For children who know the alphabet and are eager to begin reading.

Reading with Help   Preschool–Grade 1
• basic vocabulary • short sentences • simple stories
For children who recognize familiar words and sound out new words with help.

Reading on Your Own   Grades 1–3
• engaging characters • easy-to-follow plots • popular topics
For children who are ready to read on their own.

Reading Paragraphs   Grades 2–3
• challenging vocabulary • short paragraphs • exciting stories
For newly independent readers who read simple sentences with confidence.

Ready for Chapters   Grades 2–4
• chapters • longer paragraphs • full-color art
For children who want to take the plunge into chapter books but still like colorful pictures.

STEP INTO READING® is designed to give every child a successful reading experience. The grade levels are only guides; children will progress through the steps at their own speed, developing confidence in their reading.

Remember, a lifetime love of reading starts with a single step!

For Christine, Beth,
and Scott
—B.W.

Visit us on the Web!
StepIntoReading.com
randomhouse.com/kids

Educators and librarians, for a variety of teaching tools, visit us at
RHTeachersLibrarians.com

ISBN 978-0-385-37400-2 (trade) — ISBN 978-0-385-37401-9 (lib. bdg.) —
ISBN 978-0-385-37402-6 (ebook)

Printed in the United States of America 10 9 8 7 6 5 4 3 2 1

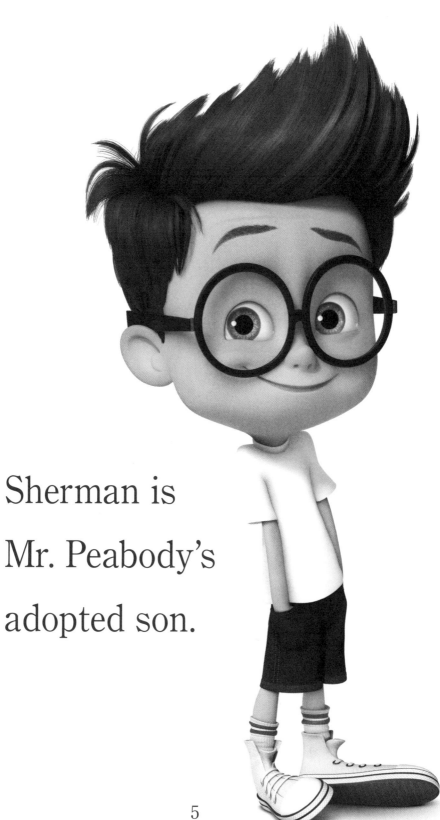

Sherman is
Mr. Peabody's
adopted son.

Mr. Peabody invented
a time-travel machine
called the WABAC.

He and Sherman visit

places in the past.

Sometimes they get
into trouble!

Sherman was supposed
to keep the time machine
a secret, but he broke
the rules.

He took his friend
Penny back in time
to ancient Egypt.

The young King Tut
wants to make
Penny his queen!
She does not want
to marry King Tut.

Mr. Peabody
and Sherman help
Penny escape.

Next, they go to Italy.
They meet the artist
Leonardo da Vinci.

Penny and Sherman
take his flying machine
for a ride!

Leonardo is surprised.
His flying machine
actually flies!

On the way home,
the time machine
crash-lands in
ancient Troy.
The Greek army is
sneaking into the city
inside a wooden horse.

Sherman joins
the Greek army
Mr. Peabody does not
think it is a good idea.

Mr. Peabody is right!
The battle is scary.
Sherman does not like
the fighting.

The wooden horse
catches fire
and rolls through Troy.

Penny is trapped
inside the wooden horse!
She yells for help.

Mr. Peabody
and Sherman
ride to the rescue.
They save Penny!

The wooden horse falls
over a cliff.
Mr. Peabody falls
with it!

Sherman knows
what to do!
He and Penny go back
to the present for help.

Sherman takes
the WABAC
through time.

Oh, no!
Sherman from the past
meets Sherman
from the present!

Mr. Peabody knows
this means trouble.

The two Shermans touch
and become one Sherman.

Then the universe starts to come apart!

Mr. Peabody, Sherman,
and Penny
have to do something!
They run
to the time machine.

They blast off

and save the universe!